GROW YOUR OWN

Esther Hall

MACMILLAN
CHILDREN'S
BOOKS

Sidney Bean and his mum lived
a busy life in a busy city.

For Finn and Alice,
and a big THANK YOU to Jamie
E.H.

First
published 2011
by Macmillan Children's Books
a division of Macmillan Publishers Limited
20 New Wharf Road, London N1 9RR
Basingstoke and Oxford
Associated companies throughout the world
www.panmacmillan.com

ISBN: 978-0-230-74794-4 (HB)
ISBN: 978-0-330-52498-8 (PB)

1 3 5 7 9 8 6 4 2

A CIP catalogue record for this book
is available from the British Library.

Printed in Belgium by Proost

Every day Mum put on her grey clothes, walked Sidney to school, and went to work in a big grey building.

Every evening dinnertime arrived with a **PING**,

came out of boxes,

and was eaten off knees.

The nearest Sidney came to a vegetable was a mushroom on his pizza — and he usually picked that off!

Until one summer holiday, when Sidney
went to stay with his Granny Milner
and her dog Vincent in the countryside.

"It's going to be a grand summer, Sidney," said Granny. "I think we'll do a bit of work in the vegetable patch."
Sidney put on his wellington boots.

"You weed, I'll feed," said Gran, as she spread pongy manure around the soil.

"Eugh! What's this, Granny?" said Sidney.
"It looks like Martian food!"

"Oooh! That's broccoli young Sid, and
it will put muscles where you didn't
know you had them," said Granny.

That evening Sidney and his gran had broccoli and pasta bake for dinner. Sidney didn't think it was that bad, for Martian food.

After his bath Sidney climbed into bed.
He ached from head to toe.
It must have been from all the digging . . .

or were his muscles really **growing?**

The next morning Sidney and Granny set to work planting peppers and digging up carrots.

"Yuck!"
said Sidney.

"These carrots are all covered in poo, Gran. I'm not eating those!"
"Oooh! It's only a bit of soil Sidney. We'll wash them off, and they'll help you see in the dark."

Sidney had to admit that honey-roasted carrots were rather nice . . .

although that night he still needed his torch to read under the covers.

Sidney woke to the sound of a squeaky wheelbarrow. He hurried outside to see what **Gran** was doing.

"Erm, what are these long green things, **Gran**?"
"They're runner beans, **Sid**," said **Gran**. "They're full of energy and will help you run as fast as the wind."

Sidney helped Granny to make
a tasty bean stew for dinner.
That evening he raced Vincent
down the track.

Sid certainly felt faster and there was
definitely something a bit windy about him!

It rained heavily that night, but the next morning
was dry and warm.
"Oooh!" said Granny Milner. "That rain
has worked its magic, Sid. Look
at all these juicy strawberries!
They'll put colour in your cheeks!"

Sidney picked a great bowlful, and he, Gran and Vincent ate every last one.

When Sid looked in the mirror that night,
he certainly did have rosy cheeks.

But it could have been a bit of strawberry juice.

Sidney and his granny worked hard that summer,

digging up veg and picking fruit.

Every day Sidney tried something new to eat.

One day they even set up a stall outside the cottage to sell all the extra fruit and veg they couldn't eat. They sold out in no time at all.

"I've just had a smashing idea, Sid," Granny said.
But when Sidney asked what it was, Gran just smiled. "Wait and see," she said.

The summer flew by. Soon it was time for Sidney to head back to the city. He couldn't wait to see his mum! As they waited, Granny busied herself filling boxes with fruit and veg.

Sid told Gran that they wouldn't all fit into Mum's little car. "Wait and see," smiled Gran.

Vincent barked at the sound of an engine and Sidney rushed outside to see . . .

. . . his mum, in her new delivery van!

Sidney and Mum went back to the city.

Sidney's mum was still busy, but Sid helped
with her deliveries whenever he could.

Mum didn't go to work in the big grey building any more,

and they gave the microwave away to the lady next door.

Every weekend they went to help Granny and Vincent in the garden.

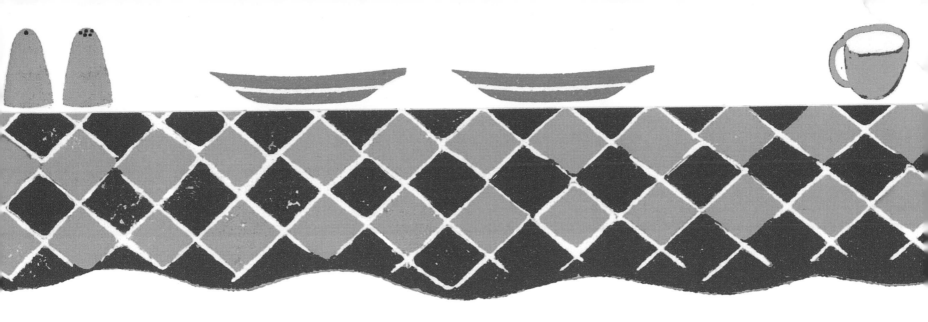

Oooh yes, Sidney really loved his fruit and veg.
Well, all except . . .

. . . mushrooms!